*I dedicate this book to my daughters, Chloe and Ava Collier,
who worked so hard as the star models for this project.*

*Even though we all were in the midst of a pandemic, they displayed great energy
and expression and reflected the wonderful message from the book, which is:
Once you discover your rainbow, strive to be a rainbow for someone else.*

ABOUT THIS BOOK

The illustrations for this book were done in watercolor and collage on 300 lb. Arches cold-pressed watercolor paper, then floated on canvas. This book was edited by Alvina Ling and designed by Véronique Lefèvre Sweet and Christine Kettner. The production was supervised by Nyamekye Waliyaya, and the production editor was Andy Ball. The text was set in Caslon Antique, and the display type is Brandon Printed Double.

MUSIC

IS A

RAINBOW

Bryan Collier

(L B)

LITTLE, BROWN AND COMPANY
NEW YORK BOSTON

It was early morning, the only alone time the boy had with his father.
He would watch as Daddy read the newspaper and sipped his cup of coffee.

Daddy would always pretend to be surprised when he caught sight of the boy in the doorway, but of course he knew he was there the whole time.

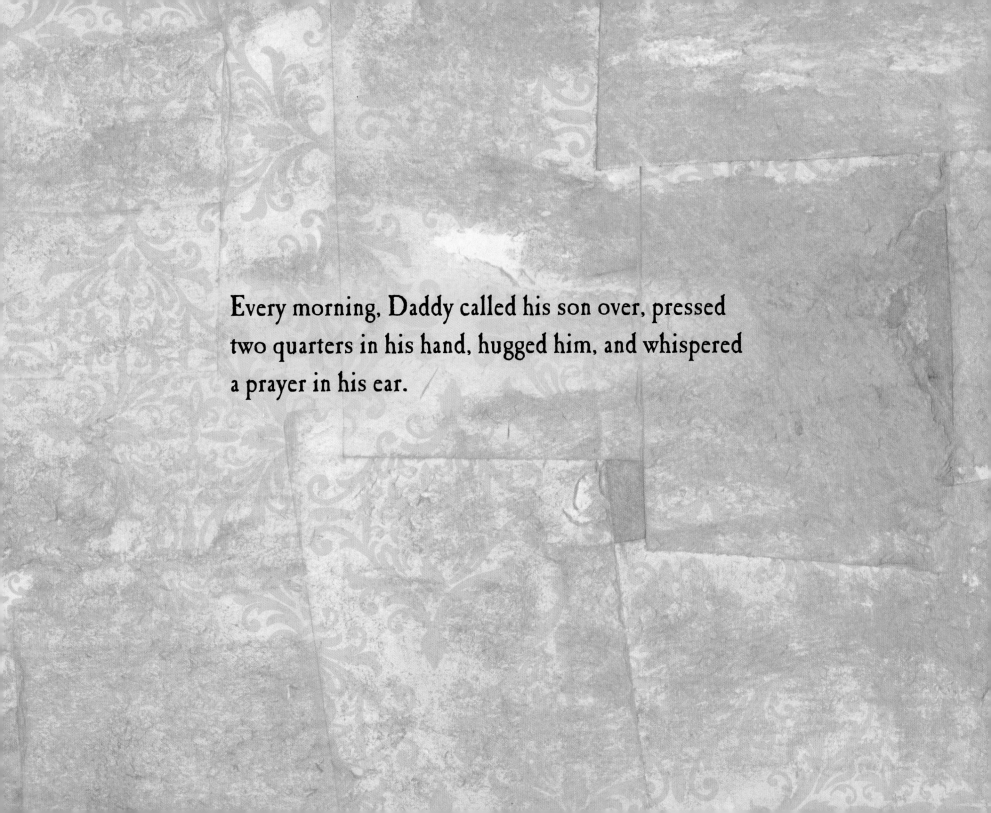

Every morning, Daddy called his son over, pressed two quarters in his hand, hugged him, and whispered a prayer in his ear.

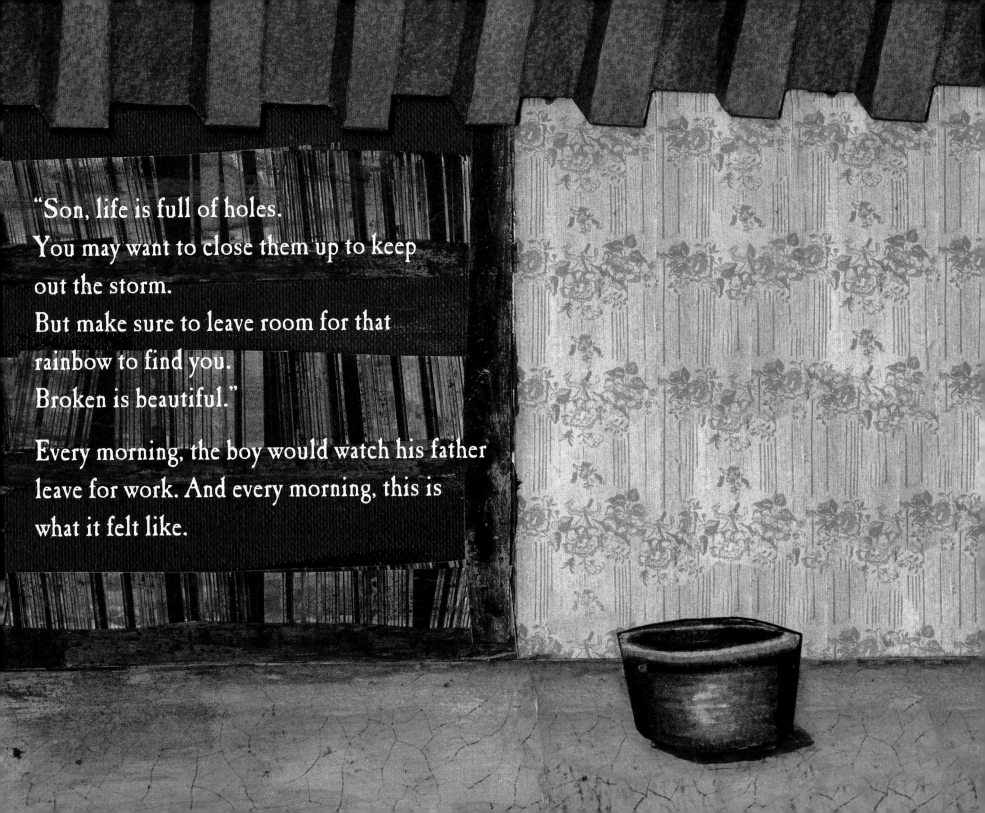

"Son, life is full of holes.
You may want to close them up to keep
out the storm.
But make sure to leave room for that
rainbow to find you.
Broken is beautiful."

Every morning, the boy would watch his father
leave for work. And every morning, this is
what it felt like.

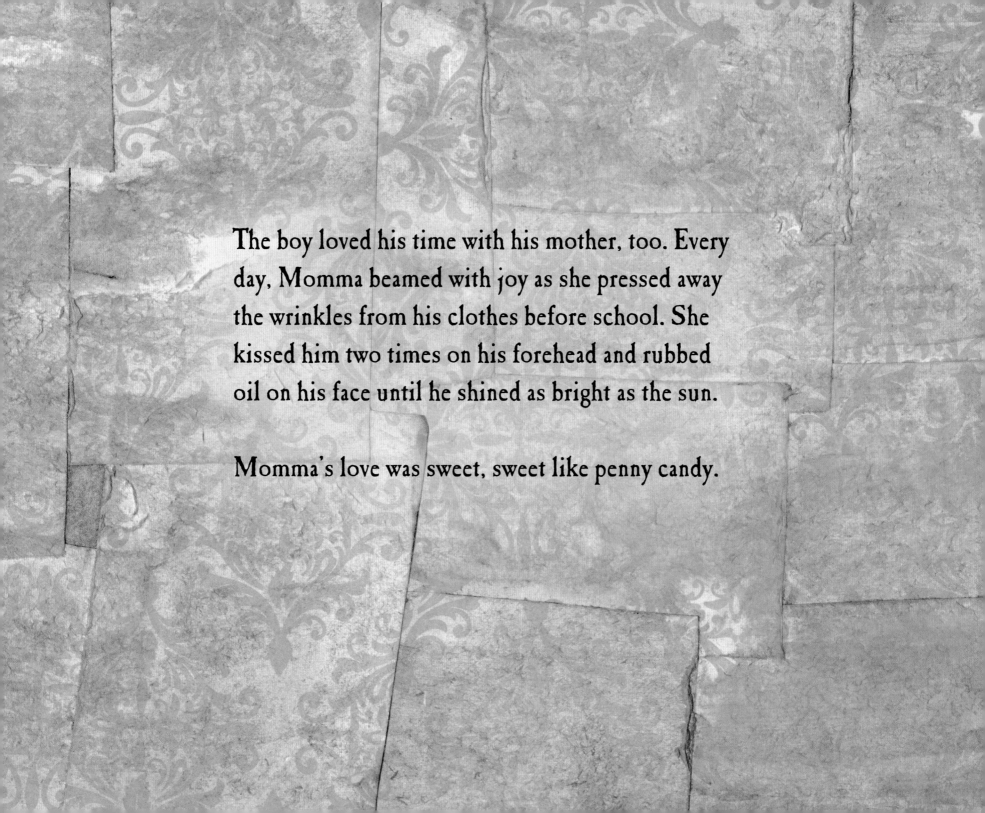

The boy loved his time with his mother, too. Every
day, Momma beamed with joy as she pressed away
the wrinkles from his clothes before school. She
kissed him two times on his forehead and rubbed
oil on his face until he shined as bright as the sun.

Momma's love was sweet, sweet like penny candy.

But on his seventh birthday, something went wrong.

Momma got sick.
Daddy said she had to go
away for a while.

And this is what it felt
like to the boy.

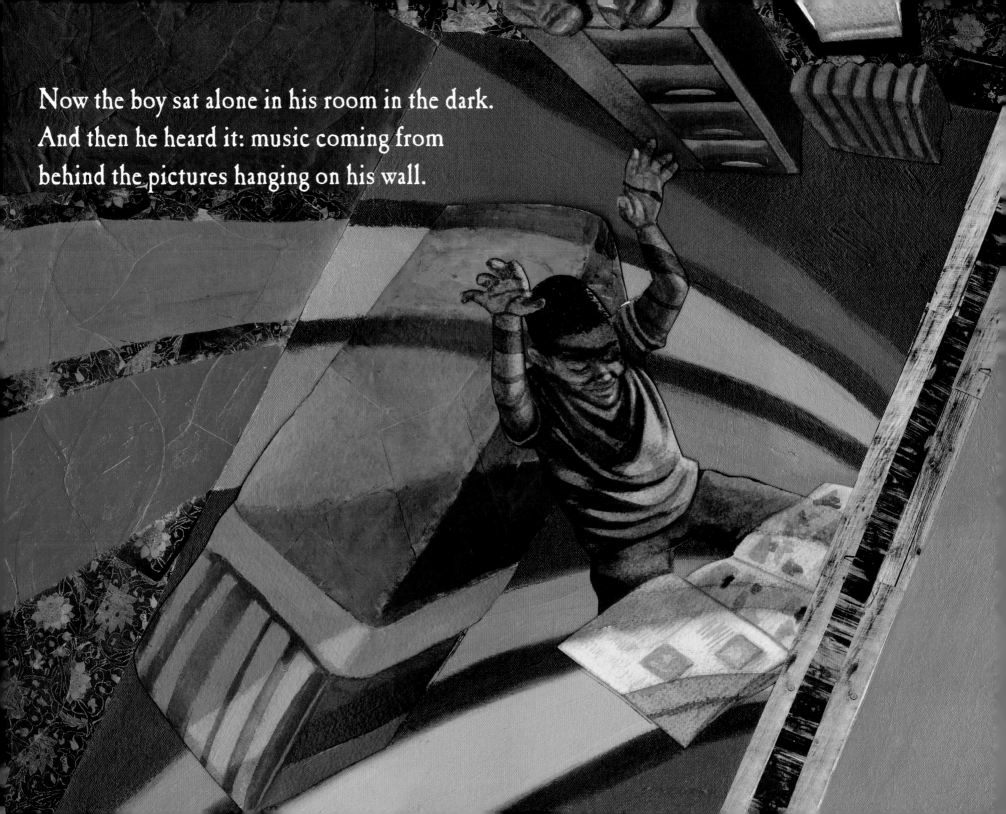

Now the boy sat alone in his room in the dark.
And then he heard it: music coming from
behind the pictures hanging on his wall.

Suddenly, the boy could relax in the blue and green. He could shine in the yellow and red, and he could dream in the purple and pink.

And like his daddy's hugs and his momma's kisses on his forehead, music was a rainbow—a rainbow of love.

But that feeling didn't last for long.

Because his friends were outside waiting for him to get into trouble.

Known in the streets as the South Side bandits, they would sneak into ice cream trucks and go joy riding! They were eager to get into more mischief.

But as soon as he discovered the movie theater, something in his head and heart said, *Stop!* So he did.

Now the boy sat alone in the theater in the dark.
He loved the smell of buttery popcorn.

When the movie began, the music started, too.
The boy closed his eyes and saw the purple, red, yellow,
and green light that chased all that darkness away.

The boy could relax. He could shine, and he could dream.

And the music was love. Love like Daddy's hugs
and Momma's kisses on his forehead.

But that feeling didn't last for long.

One day, bored and hungry, he and the boys got an idea.

They broke into the rec center through a half-opened window in the back of an alley.

With no real plan, they just ripped and ran from one room to another to another, until someone discovered the pantry cupboard where all the goodies were stored.

Food fight!

But then he found a room with a piano, and something in his head and heart said, *Stop!* So he did.

On the piano he hit one white key, and then he hit all the white keys. One by one, he hit all the black keys, too, loving the sound each key made.

He combined the sounds by running his fingers from the highest, softest notes, like Momma's voice, to the lowest and deepest notes, like Daddy's voice.

The boy could relax. He could shine, and he could dream.

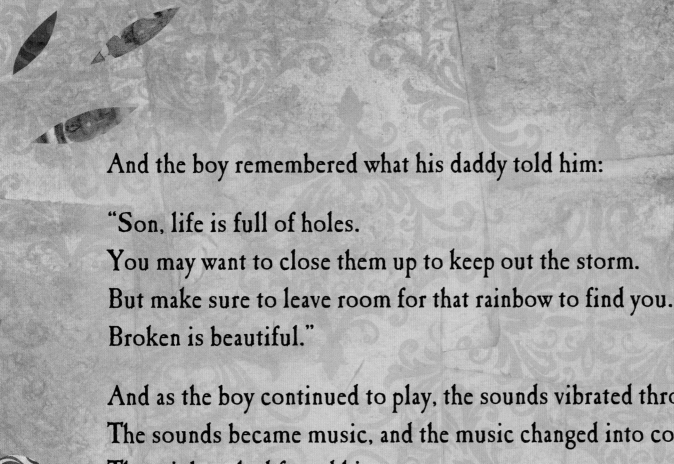

And the boy remembered what his daddy told him:

"Son, life is full of holes.
You may want to close them up to keep out the storm.
But make sure to leave room for that rainbow to find you.
Broken is beautiful."

And as the boy continued to play, the sounds vibrated through his body.
The sounds became music, and the music changed into colors.
The rainbow had found him.

And then that feeling lasted forever.

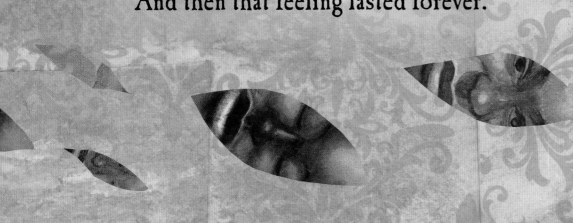

AUTHOR'S NOTE

This book was inspired by three main elements: world-class poet, artist, and activist Maya Angelou; the well-known poem "The Road Not Taken" by beloved American poet Robert Frost; and supernova Quincy Jones, a renowned musician, producer, and humanitarian.

The thread that connects all these sources of inspiration for me is the choices one makes when faced with life's storms or dark places.

Time after time, the boy discovers that music is his light or rainbow in the midst of darkness.

This book was painted in watercolor and collage on canvas and tells the story of an African American boy confronted with feelings of abandonment when his father leaves for work every morning and when his mother falls ill. He discovers music, and music is his rainbow.

Peer pressure from his friends puts a cloud on him to do bad things on the street, but the boy takes a different road and chooses music, and music is his rainbow.

Even if a story starts out so sad that you'll want to cry a river wetter than tears, God always puts a rainbow in the clouds.

Thank you, Maya Angelou, Robert Frost, and Quincy Jones.

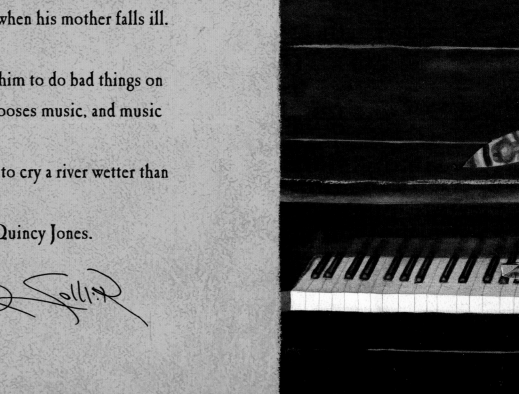